Joe and Betsy the Dinosaur

Story and pictures by
Lillian Hoban

HarperCollins*Publishers*

Joe and Betsy the Dinosaur
Copyright © 1995 by Lillian Hoban
Manufactured in China. All rights reserved.
For information address HarperCollins Children's Books,
a division of HarperCollins Publishers,
10 East 53rd Street, New York, NY 10022.

Library of Congress Cataloging-in-Publication Data
Hoban, Lillian.
    Joe and Betsy the dinosaur / story and pictures by Lillian Hoban.
        p.   cm. — (An I can read book)
    Summary: Although Joe's pet dinosaur Betsy is too big for some activities,
a formidable task allows her to demonstrate that sometimes bigger is better.
    ISBN 0-06-024473-9. — ISBN 0-06-024474-7 (lib. bdg.)
    ISBN 0-06-444209-8 (pbk.)
    [1. Dinosaurs—Fiction.   2. Size—Fiction]   I. Title.
PZ7.H635Jo   1995   93-44725
[E]—dc20   CIP
                                                                      AC

13 SCP 10
❖

For Kobi and Ilana,
the two newest stars
—L.H.

Joe and his pet dinosaur, Betsy,

lived in a cave.

On nice days
they played tag
with their friends
on the plain.

6

On rainy days

they played hide-and-seek

with their friends

in the forest.

9

One day it snowed,

and none of their friends

came out to play.

"Now what can we do?" asked Betsy.

"All of our friends are staying

snug and warm at home."

11

"We could visit them,"

said Joe.

"Maybe their mommas and poppas

will invite us in,

and we can be

snug and warm too."

So Joe and Betsy put on

their mufflers and hats

and went visiting.

First they went to visit

the Lion family.

On the way,

they came to a hill

near a pond.

14

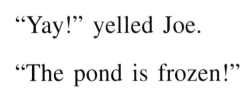

"Yay!" yelled Joe.

"The pond is frozen!"

16

He ran down the hill

and went slipping and sliding

over the ice.

He twirled round and round.

"This is fun," he called.

"You try it, Betsy."

Betsy slid down the hill.

KERPLUNK!

The ice broke

into a thousand pieces.

Big chunks flew up in the air.

Icy water rained down.

"Uh oh!" said Joe.

"I forgot how big you are."

"I'm all wet," said Betsy.

"Maybe Momma and Poppa Lion

will let you dry off

near their fire," said Joe.

When they came to the Lions' den
they heard snarling and roaring
and crashing and bashing.

"The children must be having fun,"
said Joe.

Betsy stepped up to the door
and knocked.

CRASH!

BANG!

Betsy's big feet
broke through the steps.

"Oh no!" said Joe.

BAM!

The door fell down.

Poppa Lion stuck his head out.

"Now look what you've done!"

he said.

"It's Joe and Betsy!"

called the little Lion children.

"Let them in!

Let them in!"

"I will not,"

said Poppa Lion.

"Betsy is too big,

and there are too many

in here already!"

called Momma Lion.

"I think we better come back

some other time,"

said Joe.

"That's right,"

said Poppa.

"Come back

when you can play outside."

He picked up the door

and slammed it shut.

"I'm cold," said Betsy.

"I thought we were going to be snug and warm."

"Let's visit the Bear family," said Joe.

"Maybe they will invite us in for tea and honey."

"Yum," said Betsy.

When they got to the Bears' den,

it was very quiet.

"It looks like no one is home,"

said Joe.

"There is smoke coming
from the chimney," said Betsy.
"I will see if they have
the kettle on."

She rested her chin

on the chimney and looked down.

Smoke tickled her nose.

KERCHOO!

Betsy sneezed, and

the chimney tumbled down.

"Uh oh!" said Joe.

SLAM!

The roof caved in.

"Oh no!" said Joe.

"Wa! Wa! Wa!"

a baby cub wailed.

Momma Bear stuck her head

through the hole in the roof.

"You woke up the baby!"

she said, and growled.

"Just when he fell asleep!"

"Go play someplace else,"

yelled Poppa Bear.

"You're too big

for your own good!"

"Maybe we better go home,"

said Joe.

So Joe and Betsy

went back to their cave.

It was cold

and it was damp

and it was not a bit cozy.

"I wish I could make a fire,"

said Joe,

"but we have no wood."

"The forest is full of trees,"

said Betsy.

"Trees are wood."

"Trees are very big,"

said Joe.

"You need small pieces of wood

to make a fire."

39

"I can make small pieces

out of big trees,"

said Betsy.

"How?" asked Joe.

"Watch me," said Betsy.

She went outside and sat down

on top of an old, dead tree.

CRACK!

The tree fell over.

Betsy whacked the big branches
with her tail.

THWOCK!

They broke into logs.

She grabbed a log in her jaws.

CRUNCH!

It broke into little sticks.

"Now we have lots of small pieces
of wood," said Betsy.

"They are just right

for making a fire!" cried Joe.

Joe rubbed two sticks together.

He rubbed and rubbed

until smoke came out.

44

Then he blew on the smoke

until fire came out.

He piled logs on the fire

until it burned brightly.

Joe hugged Betsy.

"You did a good job,"

he said.

"I am glad you are big."

"Yes," said Betsy.

"Sometimes big is better."

"Now let's make a pot of tea,"

said Joe.

"Yum," said Betsy.

Joe and Betsy sat

near the fire

and drank their tea.

And they were toasty warm

and cozy together.